s novel is entirely a work of fiction. The names, characters and
dents portrayed in it are the work of the author's and illustrator's
ginations. Any resemblance to actual persons, living or dead, events
ocalities, is entirely coincidental.

ished by EVA BOOKS 2021 – c/o Harry King Films Limited
　　　　　　　　　　　　　1&2 The Barn
　　　　　　　　　　　　　West Stoke Road
　　　　　　　　　　　　　Lavant
　　　　　　　　　　　　　n/r Chichester
　　　　　　　　　　　　　West Sussex PO18 9AA

right © NP Sercombe 2022

rights of Nicholas Sercombe to be identified as the author of this
have been asserted in accordance with the Copyright, Designs and
ts Act 1988.

P catalogue record for this book is available from the British
y.

978-1-8381045-6-6 (Hardback)

ayout & cover design by Clare Brayshaw.

llustration by Juliet Snape.

Bruce Old Style.

d and printed by: York Publishing Services Ltd
field Road, Layerthorpe, York YO31 7ZQ

904 431213

www.yps-publishing.co.uk

ts reserved. No part of this publication may be reproduced,
n a retrieval system, or transmitted, in any form or by any
y that we mean electrical, mechanical, photocopying, recording
wise, without the prior written permission of the publisher.

k is sold subject to the condition that it shall not, by way of
otherwise, be lent, re-sold, hired out or otherwise circulated
he publisher's prior written consent in any form of binding
other than that in which it is published and without similar
　including this condition being imposed on the subsequent

THE UNEXPURGATED MEMOIRS

SHERLOCK HOLMES

BOOK 13

THE RELISH OF RAMPANT ROD

by NP Sercombe

The un-edited manuscript originally
The Adventure of Silver Blaze writt
Dr. John Watson and Sir Arthur Con

Illustrations by Juliet Sna

THE UNEXPURGATED ADVENTURES OF SHERLOCK HOLMES

Books in the Series:

A BALLS-UP IN BOHEMIA
THE MYSTERIOUS CASE OF MR. GINGERNUTS
THE CASE OF THE RANDY STEPFATHER
MY FIRST PROPER RURAL MURDER
THE ORANGES OF DEATH!
THE MAN WITH THE HAIRY FACE
A GANDER AT THE BLUE CARBUNCLE
THE SPECKLED BAND SPECULATION
THE ADVENTURE OF THE ENGINEER'S TONGUE
THE MYSTERIOUS MARRIAGE OF THE GAY BACHELOR
THE SECRET PREDICAMENT OF THE STUPID BANKER
THE ADVENTURES OF THE PSYCHEDELIC TREES

THE UNEXPURGATED MEMOIRS OF SHERLOCK HOLMES

Books in the Series:

THE RELISH OF RAMPANT ROD

Nicholas Sercombe is a writer and producer for film and television. He has been lucky enough to work in comedy for most of the Holocene period with some of the greatest performers and writers. He is most comfortable when reading Conan Doyle and even happier when re-writing these extraordinarily entertaining stories by Dr. John Watson.

Juliet Snape studied illustration at Cambridge School of Art and Central St. Martins. She has illustrated over 100 books and her work has been published around the world.

She is a fan of Sherlock Holmes – her father even lived in Baker Street – and, in the words of Conan Doyle, she is *"naturally gravitated to London, that great cesspool into which all the loungers and idlers of the Empire are irresistibly drained."* She lives in London and loves sketching, finding inspiration all around her. She has two children, both successful creatives.

For lovers of horses, horseracing and gambling on the turf

The Relish of Rampant Rod

(published in The Strand *in December 1892 with the title 'THE ADVENTURE OF SILVER BLAZE'*
by Dr. Watson and Arthur Conan Doyle)

'I shall have to go down,' said Holmes, as we sat down together to our breakfast one morning.

'Isn't that what one of the Siamese twins said to you last night?'

'It was, Watson, and indeed she did, but this is in a different context. Tsk! I mean to go down to Dartmoor, not Mother Kelly's knocking shop. To King's Pyland.'

At last, he was on his way. There was but one problem facing us presently and that was the singular disappearance of Rampant Rod, the indomitable racehorse that was both the Guineas and Derby winner – by five lengths, no less – and the even money favourite for the St. Leger to be run next Wednesday. Indeed, my only wonder was that my companion had not already been mixed up in this extraordinary case, which was the one topic of conversation through the length and breadth of England, and we were in it up to our necks.

'Tell me, Watson, what level of liability do we have on this horse?'

'Almost every single penny that we have. Eight guineas and ten shillings, Holmes, the wager placed before the disappearance. If Rampant Rod doesn't turn up for the Leger, we are in Queer Street! Nifty Nigel has a reputation for never refunding wagers.'

'Nasty Nige of the Old Kent Road?'

I nodded. Holmes muttered an indistinguishable babble of "shyster" and "carbuncle on society" and other unreportable opinions about turf accountants. He looked up at me. 'Fear not, Watson. I am on the case.'

This appeared to be true. For the whole morning my companion had rambled about the room with his chin upon his chest and his brows knitted, charging, and re-charging his pipe with the strongest black tobacco, and absolutely deaf to any of my questions or remarks. Fresh editions of every paper had been sent up by our newsagent only to be glanced over and tossed down into a corner. Yet, silent as he was, I knew perfectly well what it was that he had been brooding over. On top of the missing wonder-horse there was the tragic murder of its trainer. When, therefore, the great detective suddenly announced his intention of setting out for the scene of the drama, it was only what I had both expected and hoped for.

'I know something about horses, Holmes, and I would be most happy to go down to Dartmoor with you, if I should not be in the way, but I am expecting a friend to visit me this afternoon. Well, I say he is a friend, but I think it would be better to label him an old army chum from my Kabul days in the 66th Berkshire Foot. He is a freshly made-up colonel.'

'Indeed? And therefore I suspect the name of this fellow is Sandy.'

'No, Holmes, contrary to your theorem, not every officer in the army is called Sandy.'

-2-

'None of them are called Sandy by birth, Watson. In the strange ways of the army evolved over generations, Sandy will become his name.'

'Oh, what complete bollocks, Holmes! He is Archie. Archibald Tugwell. A crown says that he isn't called Sandy.'

I slapped down a silver coin onto the regency sideboard, our customary spot to place ongoing wagers struck between us. It was a half crown only, hoping he would not notice; quite simply, I didn't have any more money.

'Five shillings to me. Will you never learn my perspicacity as a top detective?'

He stood up. He rifled his pockets for cash, of which there seemed to be a pitiful dearth. He withdrew a shilling, two sixpences, a threepence, a groat and an old fly-button and slammed them down onto the polished mahogany. He sat down again.

'I can tell you now that whatever it is in that hotchpotch you lay down, Holmes, you have lost.'

'Well, it is all I have left, Watson, until this ruddy horse turns up. Why do you fuss so?'

'Because I have won already. I know Archie well. He is susceptible to nicknames but will not tolerate them. During our time together in India and Afghanistan he was once called Verruca, a childish derivation of his second Christian name, Vereker. But only briefly, because Archie set to the stylist with his fists and the imbecilic moniker was soon forgotten. So, there you go Holmes, the chances of him being called Sandy at some point in his army career are decent enough but it wouldn't be for very long.'

'A fellow pugilist! But is that it?' said Holmes, lifting his brows and napkin simultaneously.

'Why, yes? There is nothing else to add. Archie's imminent arrival puts paid to my journey to Kings Pyland.'

'Thank God for that!'

What was this? He didn't want me as his travelling companion and *auteur*? This was very unsettling! I had given up my occupation as a general practitioner and devoted my life to compiling the Sherlock Holmes chronicles. The look on Holmes's face told me that my distress must have been prominently projected in my features.

'Don't look so sour, Watson. I don't mean it. Truthfully, I find it a pity, my dear friend, as you would confer a great favour upon me by coming.'

I mustered a wan smile. Not only was I the reporter of each adventure but I was also the architect of his burgeoning reputation as the country's finest private detective. Admittedly, the country's *only* private detective. Moreover, I was his sounding-board for his thoughts, theories, and deductions, delivered schoolmaster-to-pupil. Just where would he be without me?

'There are points about this case,' said he, 'which promise to make it an absolutely unique one. I have, I think, to make my way first to Paddington station and... WHO is that?'

Holmes was interrupted by a sharp rap of knuckles on the door. We both looked over to the vestibule. The knock was followed by a muffled whimper and repeated slapping of palms. Once more, the great detective knitted his brows. I jumped up and opened it. To my amazement, Mrs. Hudson stumbled in backwards, as if she had been leaning against the other side, with my old army chum lurching in behind her in a very disabled fashion. With small cries of distress, they both tripped over their feet, lost their balance and, whilst he threw me a glance mid-flight, shouted "What ho, Boner!" and they landed on top of each other.

'Archie!' cried I.

'Sandy?' cried Holmes.

The cheat!

'Yes?' cried our intruder, thus losing my wager.

Holmes collected up the coins and gave the half a crown a dismissive glance before he pocketed the lot.

'All is fair in love and gambling,' the nickname sleuth announced. 'And your friend is making a fine impression of a champion wrestler.' He moved into my personal space and looked me straight in the eye, like an owl. 'And Boner?'

The sound of my best friend uttering this bygone name made my heart skip. I had no wish to hark back to my army days in Afghanistan, and so I forced a smile and swivelled my eyes down to my crotch.

'It is nothing to do with that, Holmes,' said I.

'I know that Watson!' he hissed, wearing a grin like a chimpanzee locked in a banana shop. 'It is a childishly simple derivative of army slang for a medical officer: Sawbones. Anyone could tell you that.'

Spot on! But I couldn't let him get away with it. 'No, Holmes, you are wrong. It is, er, a hook of extreme sophistication, which emerged from a knit of companion officers, er...united in brotherhood, er... on foreign

My army chum had never bothered with foreplay.

manoeuvres… seeking valour… in the face of a worthy adversary in the brutal form of the Afghan hillman.'

'Is that so?' said he, turning away to watch Archie clamber onto our landlady and slide into a double body pinion, which was highly reminiscent of my father's ferrets mating. I joined Sherlock Holmes by his side. He was fixated.

'Mrs. Hudson seems to be remarkably indulgent of your friend. She must like him.'

'Girls don't just like Archie, Holmes, they *love* him!' I bent down and jabbed a finger of envy. 'In Kabul you would be more likely to find him in this sort of situation than asleep, which is why he was known as…'

'Sandy. Sandy being the short name for sandwich,' sniffed Holmes, with a distinct air of contentment. 'He was always the filling.'

'Brilliant, Holmes!' I ejaculated. 'Masterful!'

It was at this moment that London's most entrepreneurial property developer must have realised that her reputation was on the line. She heaved her bonny knee into Sandy's danglies. Poor Archie! He racked his back in agony and screamed: 'Jumping jizz jobbers!' as Holmes and I sucked teeth harmoniously. Mrs. Hudson released herself with an easy shove to one side, stood up sprightly, dusted her hands, gave us a rueful, cheeky harrumph and marched out of the apartment.

Meanwhile, what was left of my chum lay curled up on the Azerbaijani prayer mat, nursing his nethers, and groaning in defeat. Rather him than me…

'Bloody hell, this rug stinks!'

'Don't you remember? The natives baptise every new prayer mat by having a waz on it.'

'I would if I could, but thanks to your Mrs. Hudson's kneecap my chap is hiding somewhere near my exhaust pipe.'

'Enough of this ribaldry, Watson! Your friend has arrived in the nick of time. We have, I think, just time to catch our train from Paddington. Bring him with you. I will go further into the matter of Rampant Rod upon our journey. You would oblige me by bringing with you your very excellent field glasses.'

I gave Archie my hand and helped him to his feet. I reached into the Napoleon escritoire for the binoculars, which were positioned next to the Manstopper. I was in the deepest trepidation of having to use the revolver ever again after my fractured wrists had only just mended themselves.* Still, I couldn't resist the urge to put the wind up my old army chum. I whisked it out and pointed it straight at him pulling the hammer back with my thumb. I must tell you, dear adventure-enthusiast, if you could have seen the way that Archie jumped sideways, his eyes bulging like a bullfrog in a French chef's garden! Once I had stopped laughing, I replaced it inside the Napoleon's drawer. We left the apartment in the great detective's wake. The game was afoot!

* * *

---

* see *The Adventure of The Psychedelic Trees*

And so it happened that an hour or so later I found myself in the corner of a first-class carriage compartment, a third-class ticket in my pocket, flying along, *en route* for Exeter, while Sherlock Holmes, with his sharp eager face framed in his ear-flapped travelling-cap – what we called *The Lestrade* – dipped rapidly into the bundle of fresh papers which he had procured at Paddington station. We had left Reading far behind us before he thrust the last of them under the seat and offered me his cigar-case.

'We are going well,' said he. 'Here, take one of these and puff hard. And you, Colonel Tugwell. I work upon the theory that if we make enough of a fug in the compartment, the guard will overlook us on his rounds.'

'Indeed, Archie, light one up, there's a good fellow. Lord knows how many times we have been pulled up for being ticketless or found seated in a senior compartment and fined.'

All three of us lit up and puffed hard to generate as much smoke as possible.

'You make a habit of defrauding the railway?' enquired my army chum.

Sherlock Holmes glared at Archie. I made a timely interjection...

'Needs must when the devil drives, Archie,' said I. 'Most of the time we live hand to mouth. The life of a private detective and his faithful accomplice is not an occupation that pays well.'

'We live on the edge of the precipice of impecuniosity,' confirmed Holmes, 'so, mind your own business.'

Holmes stared at my army chum. He was very prickly towards Archie, regardless of his somewhat foolish observation. I sensed a clash of personalities, and there was small wonder on my part. Archie bore an air of reckless combativeness, as to be expected of a career soldier, mixed with a rich seam of self-esteem, and Holmes was used to being in the position of top dog.

Holmes resorted to looking out of the window and glancing at his watch. After a while he said: 'Watson. Make a note. Our rate at present is fifty-three and a half miles an hour.'

'I have not observed the quarter-mile posts,' said I.

'But I have,' said Archie, 'and you are spot-on, old fruit. Bravo!'

The great detective winced at the sobriquet, unaccustomed as he was to such familiarity, but especially Archie, who, on first encounter, came across as such a cock. Unfortunately, this wasn't the first time he had added a term of endearment to an observation for Sherlock Holmes. On the way to the railway station there was "my old chav;" another was "my old chum" and the last had been, would you believe it, "my old Holborn." One too many because Sherlock Holmes had lost his patience.

'*Mister* Tugwell! Kindly refrain from addressing me with niggardly epithets. You may think that you will draw me closer to you by what you perceive to be familiarity; in fact, you achieve quite the opposite. My name is Sherlock Holmes, not "old fruit." Kindly address me as *Mister* Holmes.'

Archie's features blanched and his soup-strainer bristled independently. 'So sorry to have biffed you in the shnozzle, Mister Holmes!' said Archie sarcastically and then turned away abruptly to stare out of the window.

I studied the oleaginous Archie, now looking more like his age of thirty-nine than ever before. He looked mighty uncomfortable in his seat, but then he was a tall, willowy chap, a couple of inches on the great detective and yours truly, and the railway didn't provide much leg room. He wore his red hair swept back in an irritatingly crinkle which, strangely, complimented his moustache. He had Celtic blood in his ancestry, of this there was no doubt. In Kabul, I remember him being particularly proud of his family name, often expounding his west country roots in the mess of an evening. Maybe there was some Irish in him too, his green eyes were his most prominent feature. Anyway, whatever Archie may have imagined about his heritage, the truth is that all his forbearers would have been in and out of each other's mud huts every night. Nobody would have a clue as to who was who's. All of them were related in one way or another.

'Watson!' barked Holmes shaking me out of my daydream. 'I presume you have looked into this matter of the murder of John Straker and disappearance of Rampant Rod?'

'Well, I am only a detective's companion, Holmes, but I have seen what the *Telegraph* and the *Chronicle* have to say.'

'It is one of those cases where the art of the reasoner should be used rather for the sifting of details than for the acquiring of fresh evidence. The tragedy has been so uncommon, so complete, and of such personal importance to so many people that we are suffering from a plethora of surmise, conjecture, and hypotheses. The difficulty is to detach the framework of fact – of absolute, undeniable fact – from the embellishment of theorists and reporters. Then, having established facts upon a sound basis, it is our duty to see what inferences may be drawn, and which are the special points upon which the whole mystery turns. On Tuesday evening I received a telegram from Colonel Tosser, the owner of the horse.'

'Tosser?!' I ejaculated. 'No, Holmes, that name cannot be true.'

'It is hard to believe,' he chuckled. 'But it is true. I received a second telegram from Inspector Gregory, who is looking after the case, inviting my cooperation.'

'Gregory, not Lestrade? Then why are you wearing the deerstalker? And why did you not go down yesterday?'

'Because Lestrade passed the problem to Gregory who insisted upon a day's solitude with Colonel Tosser. I respected his request.'

'I don't believe that any flat-foot from Scotland Yard would stop you, Holmes!'

'You are correct, Doctor…' whispered Holmes, with a sigh.

Archie grunted. His moustache bristled.

'Oh, yes, Colonel Tugwell, I made a blunder,' confessed Holmes. 'Contrary to public belief, I make mistakes, a more common occurrence than anyone would think who knew me through Watson's memoirs. The fact is that I could not believe it possible that the most remarkable racehorse in England could long remain concealed, especially in so sparsely inhabited a place as the north of Dartmoor. From hour to hour yesterday I expected to hear that he had been found, and that his abductor was the murderer of John Straker. When, however, another morning had come and I found that, beyond the arrest of young Fitzroy Simpson, nothing else had been done I knew that I should have been at the scene of the crime. Yet, in some ways, I feel that my time yesterday had not been wasted.'

'You have formed a theorem then?' I asked.

'At least I have a grip of the essential facts of the case. I shall enumerate them to you, for nothing clears up a case so much as stating it to another person, and I can hardly expect your cooperation if I do not show you the position from which I start.'

It was sounding-board time. I lay back against the cushions. Archie thrust a cigar case under my nose. I puffed on mine whilst Holmes, leaning forward, with his long thin forefinger checking off the points upon the palm of his left hand, gave me a sketch of the events which had led to our journey. Then, Archie did a remarkably clever thing – he blew some sweet-smelling smoke right up the great detective's arse cheeks!

'Mister Holmes, I read the papers. I know about the disappearance of Rampant Rod but I am ignorant without an insight such as yours. This morning, my behaviour has caused you to form a sour opinion of me, for which I apologise, and I would be honoured if you would enlighten me about the facts as you see them.'

Sherlock Holmes studied Tugwell through flinty eyes. Then, he turned them upon me and squinted. Suddenly, a smirk rippled across his lips and he burst forth to Archie in style.

'Rampant Rod,' said he, 'is from Isonomy stock, and is well on his way to hold as brilliant a record as his famous ancestor. In fact, maybe he will exceed it as he has won the two classics at Newmarket and Epsom, which his sire never did. He has brought in turn each of the prizes of the turf to Colonel Tosser, his fortunate owner – well, apart from the family name – and up to the time of the catastrophe he was the favourite for the St. Leger at even money. He has always been a firm favourite with the racing public, and has never yet disappointed them, so that even at short odds enormous sums of money have been laid upon him. Bookmakers and turf accountants alike are running scared. It is obvious, therefore, that there were many people who had the strongest interest in preventing Rampant Rod from being at Doncaster next Wednesday.'

'I know many people who have backed him to the hilt,' remarked Archie. 'But...'

I stopped Archie in his tracks with a pointing of my right index finger and a stern expression.

'Thank you, Watson. For your information, Colonel Tugwell, I will not be interrupted. I shall continue when you have settled down.'

The great detective gazed out of the window. He shot his cuffs and adjusted his tie. He composed himself, sitting up straight and moved his jaw around a little, as if he was chewing an imaginary humbug. Finally, he flashed his eyes at Archie, which was a warning shot to remain silent from now on.

'The fact was, of course, appreciated at King's Pyland, where the Tosser's training stable is situated. Every precaution was taken to guard the Leger favourite. The trainer, John Straker, is a retired jockey, who rode in Colonel Tosser's colours before he became too heavy for the weighing-chair. He has served the Colonel for five years as a jockey, and for seven as a trainer, and has always shown himself to be a zealous and honest servant. Under him were three lads, for the establishment was a small one, containing only four horses in all. One of the lads sat up each night in the stable, while the others slept in the loft. All three bore excellent characters. John Straker, who is a married man, lived in a small villa about two hundred yards from the stables. He has no children, keeps one maidservant, and is comfortably off. The country round is very lonely, but about half a mile to the north there is a small cluster of villas which have been built by a Tavistock contractor for the use of invalids and others who may wish to enjoy the pure Dartmoor air. Tavistock itself lies two miles to the west, while across the moor, also about two miles distant, is the larger training establishment of Capleton, which belongs to Lord Backwater, and is managed by Silas Brown. In every other direction the moor is a complete wilderness, inhabited only by a few roaming gypsies. Such was the general situation last Monday night, when the catastrophe occurred.'

I flicked my cigar absent-mindedly; instead of the ash falling away the end came off completely. It missed the compartment ashtray by half an inch, bounced off the windowsill and landed in Archie's upturned trilby. He didn't notice, such was his fascination with Holmes's account of mysterious disappearance of Rampant Rod. The poor shot, however, caught the attention of my companion, who crimped his eyes at me as if to say: "Don't say a thing, Watson!" On the basis that a joke isn't truly funny unless the victim is hurt or loses money, I agreed with him.

Archie's trilby sent smoke signals!

'On that evening the horses had been exercised and watered as usual,' continued Holmes rather more intensely, 'and the stables were locked up at nine o'clock. Two of the lads walked up to the trainer's house, where they had supper in the kitchen, while the third, Cyril Bunter, remained on guard. At a few minutes after nine the maid, Edith Baxter, carried down to the stables his supper, which consisted of a dish of curried mutton. She took no liquid, as there was a water tap in the stables, and it was the rule that the lad on duty should drink nothing else. The maid carried a lantern with her, as it was very dark, and the path ran across the open moor.'

'Pardon me for the interruption, Mister Holmes,' said Archie, sniffing the air in distress and looking around him furtively, 'but *what* is that bloody awful smell?' He looked to his left and jumped up a foot in his seat. 'JUMPING JIZZCAKES! IT'S MY BEAUTIFUL HAT!'

Sure enough, his green trilby was engulfed in orange flames. Archie leaped up from his seat and wrenched down the glass of the door. He tried to manhandle the ball of flaming felt but he snatched at it. He fumbled, picked it up, panicked, threw it up in the air and juggled. Holmes and I fell about laughing as Archie levelled it up and batted it out of the carriage, like the Doctor hitting a boundary at Lord's.

'Huzzah!' cried he.

'Boo!' cried we.

But then the wind blew it back inside! We fell about laughing once more as Archie jumped up and down on it. Once the immediate danger was over, he turned his attention to the seat fabric, which was also ablaze. He shot us a glance of withering pity as he unbuttoned his fly and used his dickeydoodah as a fire hose. Once it was out, he drew himself up, lifted the window back into position, adjusted his tie and lifted his head high – he would never let us know that he was aware of the arson – and stood still, soup-strainer bristling, until his dignity had been restored. Then he sat down and stared into the horizon.

'Anyway, what was I saying?' said Holmes. 'Oh yes, Edith Baxter. She was within thirty yards of the stables when a man appeared out of the darkness and called to her to stop. As he stepped into the circle of yellow light thrown by the lantern, she saw that he was a person of gentlemanly bearing, dressed in a grey suit of tweed with a cloth cap. He wore gaiters and carried a heavy stick with a knob on it. She was most impressed, however, by the extreme pallor of his face and by the nervousness of his manner. His age, she thought, would be rather over thirty than under it.'

'"Can you tell me where I am?" he asked. "I had almost made up my mind to sleep on the moor when I saw the light of your lantern."'

'"You are close to the King's Pyland training stables,"' she said.

'"Oh, indeed! What a stroke of luck!" he cried. "I understand that a stable boy sleeps there alone every night. Perhaps that is his supper which you are carrying to him. Now I am sure you would not be too proud to earn the price of a new dress, would you?" He took a piece of white paper folded up out of his waistcoat pocket. "See that the boy has this tonight, and you shall have the prettiest frock that money can buy."'

'She was frightened by the earnestness of his manner and ran past him to the window through which she was accustomed to hand the meals. It was already open, and Bunter was seated at the small table inside. She had begun to tell him of what had happened when the stranger came up again.'

'"Good evening," said he, looking through the window, "I want to have a word with you." The girl has sworn that as he spoke, she noticed the corner of the little paper packet protruding from his closed hand.'

'"What business have you here?"' asked the lad.

'"It's business that may put something into your pocket," said the other. "You have two horses in for the St. Leger – Rampant Rod and Screw Loose. Is it a fact that Screw Loose has been covered up and could give the other one a hundred yards in five furlongs, and that the stables have put their money on him? Let me have the straight tip, and you won't be a loser."'

'"What a cheek!" cried the lad. "You're one of those damned touts. I'll show you how we serve them in King's Pyland." He sprang up and rushed across the stable to unloose the dog. The girl fled away to the house, but as she ran, she looked back, and saw that the stranger was leaning through the window. A minute later, however, when Bunter rushed out with the hound he was gone, and though the lad ran all around the building, he failed to find any trace of him.'

'One moment...' I asked. 'Did the stable boy, when he ran out the door with the dog, leave the door unlocked behind him?'

'Excellent, Watson; excellent!' exclaimed my companion.

'The importance of that point struck me so forcibly that I sent a special wire to Dartmoor yesterday to clear the matter up. The boy locked the door before he left it. The window, I may add, was not large enough for a man to get through.'

'Cyril Bunter waited until his fellow grooms had returned, when he sent a message up to the trainer and told him what had occurred.'

'Nice one, Cyril.'

'Shut up, Watson! Straker was excited at hearing the account, although he doesn't seem to have quite realised its true significance. It left him, however, vaguely uneasy, and Mrs. Straker, waking at one in the morning, found that he was dressing. In reply to her inquiries, he said that he could not sleep on account of his anxiety about the horses, and that he intended to walk down to the stables to see that all was well. She begged him to remain at home, as she could hear the rain pattering against the windows, but despite her entreaties, he pulled on his large mackintosh and left the house.'

'Missus Straker awoke at seven in the morning, called her maid, and set off for the stables. The door was open; inside, huddled together upon a chair, Bunter was sunk in a state of absolute stupor, the favourite's stall was empty, and there were no signs of his trainer.'

'The two lads who slept in the chaff-cutting loft above the harness-room were quickly roused. They had heard nothing during the night, for they are both sound sleepers. Bunter was obviously under the influence of some powerful drug; and, as no sense could be got out of him, he was left to sleep it off while the two lads and the two women of the house ran out in search of the absentees. They still had hopes that the trainer had for some reason taken out the horse for an early exercise, but on ascending the knoll near the house, from which all the neighbouring moors were visible, they not only could see no signs of the favourite, but they perceived something which warned them that they were in the presence of a tragedy.'

'About a quarter of a mile from the stables, John Straker's overcoat was flapping from a furze bush. Immediately beyond there was a bowl-shaped depression in the moor, and at the bottom of this was found the dead body of the unfortunate trainer. His head had been shattered by a savage blow from some heavy weapon, and he was wounded in the thigh, where there was a long, clean cut, inflicted evidently by some very sharp instrument. It was clear, however, that Straker had defended himself vigorously against his assailants, for in his right hand he held a small knife, which was clotted with blood up to the handle, while in his left he grasped a red and black silk cravat, which was recognised by the maid as having been worn on the neck of the stranger who had visited the stables.'

'If you don't mind me saying, Holmes, that is obvious.'

'Shut up, Watson.'

'It's bloody obvious!' added Archie.

'You too, Colonel! Let me finish… When Bunter recovered from his stupor, he confirmed the owner of the cravat. He was equally certain that the same stranger had drugged his curried mutton while standing at the window, and so deprived the stables of a watchman.'

'Hence he went into a korma? Ha!'

'Let's hope the mutton was tandoor,' said Archie, getting into the curry idioms with verve.

'For Pete's sake!'

'But, more importantly, Mister Holmes' said Archie, 'what happened to the horse?'

'The missing horse left an abundance of evidence in the mud which lay at the bottom of the fatal hollow, showing that he had been there at the time of the struggle. But from that morning he has disappeared; and although a large reward has been offered, and all the gypsies of Dartmoor are on the alert, no news has come of him. Finally, an analysis has shown that the remains of his supper, left by the stable lad, contained an appreciable quantity of powdered opium, while the people of the house partook of the same dish on the same night without any ill effect. Those are the main facts of the case stripped of all surmises and stated as baldly as possible. I shall now recapitulate what the police have done in the matter…'

'Inspector Gregory, to whom the case has been committed, is an extremely competent officer. Was he but gifted with imagination he might rise to great heights in his profession. On his arrival he promptly found and arrested the man upon whom suspicion naturally rested. There was a little difficulty in finding him, for he was thoroughly well known in the neighbourhood. His name, it appears, was Fitzroy Simpson.'

At the mention of this name, I noticed that Archie was surprised. He saw me and composed himself in the blink of an eye. I thought to myself that maybe he knew this situation already?

'He is a man of excellent birth and education, who has squandered a fortune upon the turf, and who lives now by doing a little quiet and genteel bookmaking in the sporting clubs of London.'

'Ah! No doubt he will be acquainted with… Sir Gaylon Schwinger?'[*]

Archie blanched at the mention of Schwinger. He *did* know about this situation!

'Maybe so, Watson, but an examination of Simpson's betting-book showed that bets to the amount of five thousand pounds had been registered by him against the favourite. On being arrested he volunteered the statement that he had come down to Dartmoor in the hope of getting some information about the King's Pyland horses, and about Dessie, the second favourite, which was in the charge of Silas Brown, at the Capleton Stables. He did not attempt to deny that he had acted as described the evening before, but declared that he had no sinister designs, and had simply wished to obtain first-hand information. When confronted with the cravat he turned very pale and was utterly-butterly unable to account for its presence in the hand of the murdered man. His wet clothing showed that he had been out in the storm of the night before, and his stick, which was a Penang lawyer, weighted with lead, was such a weapon as might, by repeated blows, have inflicted the terrible injuries to which the trainer had succumbed.'

'On the other hand, there was no wound upon his person, while the state of Straker's knife would show that one, at least, of his assailants must bear his mark upon him. There you have it all in a nutshell, gentlemen, and if you can give me any light, I shall be infinitely obliged to you, but I shall take all the credit.'

---

[*] see *The Secret Predicament of The Stupid Banker*

I had listened with the greatest interest to the statement which Holmes, with characteristic clearness, had laid before us. Though most of the facts were familiar to me, I had not sufficiently appreciated their relative importance, nor their connection with each other. I looked across to Archie who had changed his mood from an air of interfering sycophant to one of pontificating observer. And I think I knew why – he had a wager staked upon the second favourite, Dessie.

'Is it not possible,' I suggested, 'that the incised wound upon Straker may have been caused by his own knife in the convulsive struggles which follow any brain injury?'

'It is more than possible; it is probable,' said Holmes. 'In that case, one of the main points in favour of the accused disappears.'

'And yet, even now, I fail to understand what the theory of the police can be.'

'I am afraid that whatever theory we state has very grave objections to it. The police imagine, I take it, that this Fitzroy Simpson, having drugged the lad, and having in some way obtained a duplicate key, opened the stable door, and took out the horse, with the intention apparently, of kidnapping him altogether. His bridle is missing, so Simpson must have put it on. Then, having left the door open behind him, he was leading the horse away over the moor, when he was either met or overtaken by the trainer. A row naturally ensued, Simpson beat the living daylights out of Straker with his heavy stick without receiving any injury from the small knife which the trainer used in self-defence, and then the thief either led the horse on to some secret hiding place, or else it may have bolted during the struggle, and now be wandering out on the moors. That is the case, m'lud, as it appears to the police. Improbable as it is, all other explanations are more improbable still.'

'Gentlemen,' said Archie, drawing himself up in his seat, 'what you have stated is most fascinating. I am only a layman in your world of detection and investigative affairs, but I have an observation, and that is: why would this Fitzroy Simpson, already described by you as of decent and genteel character, with a book of wagers set against the favourite, suddenly change his persona into a kidnapper and violent murderer? It makes no sense to me. Anyway, that is my only comment upon the situation.'

An uncomfortable silence pervaded the compartment space.

'Is that it?' murmured Holmes. He pursed his lips ever-so-slightly and flicked his eyes over to me. I received the message loud and clear – we were on a mission...

'Yes, I must agree with my companion, Archie. Is that it?'

'Well, what do you mean by "is that it?" Perhaps that is it.'

'Yes, of course you think perhaps that is it. But is that it?'

'Of course, it ruddy well is! I suppose...'

'No, Archie, you're missing the point,' said I, shifting my body forward and leaning into him, looking him straight in the eye. 'Is that it?'

'Indeed. Is that it?' confirmed Holmes, also leaning forward.

'For Christ's sakes! What are you two on about?!' And then dawn broke over my chum's features... 'Oh! I understand now. This is a little routine of yours, is it not? Something to stir me up, to unsettle me!'

I glanced at Sherlock Holmes, who was poker-faced. I sensed he was about to deal the double-bluff.

'What on Earth are you talking about, Colonel? I asked you an entirely straightforward question and you failed to answer it. Is that it?'

'I did! And, yes, now that you come to mention it, THAT IS IT!'

'Good. That's all we wanted to know.'

Archie's face was a picture, as if an invisible hand had slapped him across the cheek. We could no longer hold ourselves back and burst out laughing. I think it was the way that my companion had delivered the final line that tickled us pink. What a player Holmes was! But our mirth was not to last very long... Archie stood up suddenly, ramrod straight. He bowed at the waist, thrust his hand out, looked me straight in the eye and said: 'My dear fellow, what a perfectly splendid effort.' I found myself going sheepish whilst shaking his fin. 'And Mister Holmes,' said the recently made-up colonel, gripping the great detective's hand without so much as a blink of the eye, 'I have never been so amused. Up until now I imagined such entertainment could only be found inside the stage door of the Palladium.' Holmes went through the handshaking motions looking rather flabbergasted. Then, Archie turned on his heel like a seasoned ballet dancer and exited the compartment.

Who would have thought that Archie Tugwell could have taken *le pissoir* out of our devilment in such an artful way? I looked at Sherlock Holmes and he shot me a gawp of resignation. We, the purveyors of tantalising sarcasm, had been upstaged!

* * *

It was evening before we reached Tavistock, which lies, like the boss of a shield, in the middle of the huge circle of Dartmoor. It is a very attractive town, built upon two steep banks of a river valley, the river Tavy roaring through the centre. Two gentlemen were awaiting us at the station. One was a small, alert person, very neat and dapper, in a frock coat and gaiters, with trim little side-whiskers and an eyeglass, which was Colonel Tosser, the well-known sportsman. The other was Inspector Gregory, a man who, according to Holmes, was rapidly making his name in the English detective service. Well, I had never met him before. He was young, his face all crumpled, his features softened by fatty skin as smooth as chamois. He had an air of intensity about him, mixed with an eagerness to please.

'I am delighted that you have come down, Mister Holmes,' said Colonel Tosser. 'The Inspector here has done all that could possibly be suggested; but I wish to leave no stone unturned in trying to avenge poor Straker, and in recovering my horse.'

'There is a limited amount of time been allowed for the Inspector to make his investigation whereas I have been on the case since its first announcement. Have there been any fresh developments?' asked Holmes.

'I am sorry to say that we have made very little progress,' said the Inspector. 'Perhaps you would introduce us, Mister Holmes?'

My companion went through the formalities with Archie and me. After we made fun of him on the train, my army chum was ambling around like a chastised child, kicking his feet, with a face like a mackerel on the slab. I don't remember him being a sulker, so maybe there was more on his mind than met the eye?

'We have an open carriage outside, and as you would no doubt like to see the place before the sun goes down, we might talk it over as we drive.'

A minute later we were all seated in a comfortable landau and were rattling through the quaint old Devonshire town. Inspector Gregory was full of his case, and poured out a stream of remarks, his soft cheeks all a-wobble, while Holmes threw in an occasional question or interjection. Colonel Tosser leaned back with his arms folded and his hat tilted over his eyes, while I listened with interest to the dialogue of the two detectives Gregory was formulating his theory, which was almost exactly the same as Holmes had foretold in the train.

'The net is drawn pretty close around Fitzroy Simpson,' he remarked, 'and I believe myself that he is our man. At the same time, I recognise that the evidence is purely circumstantial, and that some new developments may upset it.'

'How about Straker's knife?'

'We have come to the conclusion that he wounded himself in his fall.'

'Doctor Watson made the same suggestion on our way down. If so, it would tell against this man Simpson.'

'Undoubtedly. He has neither a knife nor any sign of a wound. The evidence against him is certainly very strong. He had a great interest in the disappearance of the Leger favourite, he lies under the suspicion of having poisoned the stable boy, he was undoubtedly out in the storm, he was armed with a heavy stick and his cravat was found in the dead man's hand. I really think we have enough to go before a jury.'

Holmes shook his head. 'A clever counsel would tear it all to rags,' said he. 'Why should he take the horse out of the stable? If he wished to injure it, why could he not do it there? Has a duplicate key been found in his possession? What chemist sold him the powdered opium? Above all, where could he, a stranger to the district, hide a horse, and such a horse as this? What is his own explanation as to the paper which he wished the maid to give to the stable boy?'

'He says that it was a ten-pound note. One was found in his purse. But your other difficulties are not so formidable as they seem. He is not a stranger to the district. He has twice lodged at Tavistock in the summer. The opium was probably brought from London. The key, having served its purpose, would be hurled away. The horse may lie at the bottom of one of the pits or old mines upon the moor.'

'Ah! But what does he say about the cravat?'

'He acknowledges that it is his and declares that he had lost it. But a new element has been introduced into the case which may account for his leading the horse from the stable.'

Holmes pricked up his ears.

'We have found traces which show that a party of gypsies encamped on Monday night within a mile of the spot where the murder took place. On Tuesday they were gone. Now, presuming that there was some understanding between Simpson and these gypsies, might he not have been leading the horse to them when he was overtaken, and may they not have him now?'

'It is certainly possible.'

'The moor is being scoured for these gypsies. I have also examined every stable and outhouse in Tavistock, and for a radius of ten miles.'

'There is another training stable quite close, I understand?'

'Yes, and that is a factor which we must certainly not neglect. As their horse, Dessie, is second in the St. Leger betting, they can only gain from the disappearance of Rampant Rod. Silas Brown, the trainer, is known to have had large bets upon the event.'

'He is not the only one!' exclaimed Archie, out of the blue. Everyone was shaken by my army chum's outburst, particularly the Scotland Yard plod. We all looked across at him, all red-faced and sitting up straight. I thought, in the circumstances, that I had better be the first person to enquire further, Archie being somewhat my responsibility.

'Tell me, Archie, old fellow, what's up?'

'From what I hear in this carriage, from the only two men making the investigation, and all so very matter-of-fact, that there is not a hope in hell of finding Rampant Rod. And if you do, he may well be dead! Surely it is as obvious to you as it is to me, that the prime suspect is Silas Brown? He has motive; he has reason; he is perfectly situated nearby. For goodness sakes, surely, we should be heading to the man's stables right now, going through the place with a fine toothcomb and finding the horse? Gentlemen, it is the only place he can be.'

'Not so, Colonel Tugwell. We have examined the stables,' said Gregory, 'and there is nothing to connect him with the affair.'

'And nothing to connect this man Simpson with the interests of Capleton stable?'

'Nothing at all.'

'Oh…fuckety, fuck, fuck, fuck and…fiddle-de-dee!' said Archie, and then he clammed up. He turned his head away from us and looked out at the passing countryside, the assembled company surprised by the outburst and language he had used.

Sherlock Holmes was in the process of lighting his Peterson. He turned his head to study Archie through a cloud of blue tobacco smoke.

Inspector Gregory sighed – he had nothing more to add – and Holmes leaned back in the carriage. The conversation had ceased and all we could hear was the wheels rolling along the iron road. A few minutes later our driver pulled up at a neat little red-brick villa with overhanging eaves. Some distance off, across a paddock, lay a long grey-tiled outbuilding. In every other direction the low curves of the moor, bronze-coloured from the fading ferns, stretched away to the skyline, broken only by the steeples of Tavistock, and by the cluster of houses away to the westward, which marked the Capleton stables. We all sprang out, except for Holmes, who continued to lean back with his eyes fixed upon the sky in front of him, entirely absorbed in his own thoughts. It was only when I touched his arm that he roused himself with a violent start and stepped out of the carriage.

'Excuse me,' said he, turning to Colonel Tosser, who had looked at him in some surprise. 'I was daydreaming.' But there was a gleam in his eyes that I recognised and an excitement in his retort which convinced me, used as I was to his ways, that his hand was upon a clue, though I could not imagine where he had found it. He drew me to one side and leaned in. 'I reckon your Colonel Tugwell has an immense investment in the St. Leger, and it must be on the second favourite,' he whispered in my ear. 'And I think I know who laid his wagers.'

'Schwinger?'

'My dear Watson, you almost usurp me!' Before the great detective could pat me on the head Inspector Gregory was on the scene.

'Perhaps you would prefer at once to go on to the scene of the crime, Mister Holmes?' said he.

'I think that I should prefer to stay here a little and go into one or two questions of detail. Straker was brought back here, I presume?'

'Yes. The inquest is tomorrow.'

'He has been in your service some years, Colonel Tosser?'

'I have always found him to be an excellent servant.'

'I presume that you made an inventory of what he had in his pockets at the time of his death, Inspector?'

'I have the things themselves in the sitting-room if you would care to see them.'

'I should be very glad.'

We all filed into the front room and sat round the central table. We were a pretty moribund bunch, all looking hangdog. Surely, thought I, while the Inspector unlocked a square tin box and laid a small heap of things before us, we could be a little more cheerful? There was a box of vestas, two inches of tallow candle, an A.D.P. briar-root pipe, a pouch of sealskin with half an ounce of long-cut cavendish, a silver watch with a gold chain, five sovereigns in gold, an aluminium pencil-case, a few papers, and an ivory-handled knife with a very delicate inflexible blade marked Weiss & Co., London. Ah! A German knife...

'This is a very singular knife,' said Holmes, examining it. He handed it over. I don't know what got into me, but I jumped up suddenly from my seat and lifted the knife above my head.

'Vice! Vee Germans manufacture ze best veppons for ze vice, ja?' cried I, and made stabbing movements left, right and centre through the air. I waited for the appreciative laughs from my audience... but they never arrived. Sadly, my audience looked startled and distinctly unamused.

'Please sit down, Watson,' said Holmes, which I did. 'For goodness sakes, what has got into you?'

'There is such an ambience of doom around here that I was merely trying to lift the mood. Is there anything wrong with that, gentlemen?'

'The dead man is laid out upstairs, right above us? His widow by his side?'

I did not know. Oh, bugger! My heart fell into my stomach and an angel flew through the room.

Archie broke the silence, gurning his face with remorse. 'I didn't realise Straker was here. I shall go up and pay my respects to her.'

Tosser and Gregory looked on resignedly as Archie headed upstairs.

Holmes took the knife from me and examined it minutely. 'This is a very singular knife, and it is surely in your line of work, Doctor?'

'It is what we call a cataract knife,' said I.

'I thought so, and enough said. A very delicate blade devised for very delicate work. A strange thing for a man to carry with him upon a rough expedition, especially as it would not shut in his pocket. I presume, as I see bloodstains upon it, that it is the one which was found in the dead man's grasp.'

The tip was guarded by a disc of cork which we found beside his body,' said the Inspector. 'His wife tells us that the knife had lain for some days upon the dressing-table, and that he had picked it up as he left the room. It was a poor weapon, but perhaps the best that he could lay his hand on at the moment.'

'Very possible. How about these papers?'

'Three of them are receipted hay-dealers' accounts. One of them is a letter of instructions from Colonel Tosser. This other is a milliner's account for thirty-seven pounds fifteen, made out by Madame Le Mesurier, of Bond Street, to William Darbyshire.'

Holmes jumped up from his chair. 'Aye-aye! What do we have here?' remarked Holmes, glancing down the account. 'Buying woman's clothing for another man? And Madame Darbyshire had somewhat expensive tastes. Twenty-two guineas is rather a heavy price for a single costume.'

'And what would Sherlock Holmes know about the price of silk and taffeta?' enquired Colonel Tosser, rather sceptically, curling his lip.

'I shall have you know, Colonel, that I am somewhat of an expert in the world of couture,' said he. 'In fact, I have written a treatise on the subject. What is so amusing, Watson?'

It was one of those embarrassing moments when I had been caught laughing out loud, but unconsciously. Now I had Gregory and Tosser gawping at me.

'I am sorry, gentlemen, I have been taken by surprise. It is just that I have never been aware of Mister Holmes's expertise in high fashion.'

Such was the incongruity of Sherlock Holmes being a leader of fashion we all laughed together, perhaps a little too hard because the great detective sighed and reached down to his small leather suitcase. He let his long white fingers walk through some documents until he pulled one out.

'As luck would have it…' said Holmes, holding up a pamphlet for all and sundry to view. '*The Mystery of the Sacred Stitch,* in case anyone is interested?' He dropped it onto the table and my lower mandible skidded to a halt alongside.

There was a spontaneous ripple of applause as they feigned interest through embarrassment, all of them jostling for a position to get a view of its cover and the author: SNJ Holmes Esq.

'Just as well we get you out into the fresh air, Watson. Inspector, there appears to be nothing more to learn here. May we now go down to the scene of the crime?'

As we emerged from the sitting-room, Archie was walking down the staircase with a woman who I assumed to be Mrs. Straker. She was peculiar; it took me a while to take her in. She had the face of a horse, which made perfect sense as the wife of a trainer, but when she laid her hand upon the Inspector's sleeve and then turned round, her slender frame all-of-a-tremble, she had the peachy of a choirboy. She was probably beautiful, but her features were compromised by her recent trauma. Her hair may have been thick and shiny, but it was tangled by her recent horror. Her mouth may have been open and welcoming, and her red lips full, but today dulled by her recent pain. Even so, the widow Straker was a very handsome woman indeed, and I detected a glint in her eye. So did Archie, who ingratiated himself by placing an arm around her shoulders. Uh-oh, he had taken a fancy to her...

'Have you got them? Have you found them?' she panted.

'No, Missus Straker,' said Archie. 'But Mister Holmes, here, has come all the way from London with Doctor Watson to help, as did I, and we shall do all that is possible.'

'Surely, I met you at a party in Plymouth, some little time ago, Missus Straker?' said Holmes.

'No sir, you are mistaken,' said she, with a remarkable coyness for a woman just bereaved. My goodness she was cute! This had not gone unnoticed by Archie, who was standing behind me, lurid of face and tapping my shoulder discreetly.

'Dear me; why, I could have sworn to it,' pursued the great detective. 'You wore a costume of dove-coloured silk with ostrich feather trimming.'

'I never had such a dress, sir,' answered the lady with a mischievous flutter about her, arms behind her

Strangely, the widow was dressed to impress!

back and now swivelling her hips side-to-side. I could have sworn she was flirting with him!

'Ah, that quite settles it,' said Holmes; and, with an apology, he followed the Inspector outside. I followed them. Then, I realised we did not have Archie with us; I re-entered the house, extracted Archie from a clinching conversation with Missus Straker, who didn't seem at all bothered about her loss, and we embarked upon a short walk across the moor. It would take us to the place where the body had been found. When we arrived at the brink of the hollow, there was the furze bush upon which the coat had been hung. Sherlock Holmes assumed control of the investigation once again whilst the Inspector and the two colonels watched on in fascination.

'There was no wind that night, I understand,' queried he to Gregory.

'None; but very heavy rain.'

'In that case the overcoat was not blown against the furze bushes but placed there.'

'Yes, it was laid across the bush.'

'You fill me with interest. I perceive that the ground has been trampled up a good deal. No doubt many feet have been there since Monday night.'

'A piece of matting has been laid here at the side, and we have all stood upon that.'

'Excellent.'

'In this bag I have one of the boots which Straker wore, one of Fitzroy Simpson's shoes and a cast horseshoe of Rampant Rod.'

'My dear Inspector, you surpass yourself!'

Holmes took the bag and descending into the hollow he pushed the matting into a more central position. Then stretching himself upon his face and leaning his chin upon his hands he made a careful study of the trampled mud in front of him.

'Halloa!' said he, suddenly, 'what's this?'

It was a wax vesta, half burned, which was so coated with mud that it looked at first like a chip of wood.

'I cannot understand how I came to overlook it,' said the Inspector, with an expression of annoyance.

Archie stood next to me. He drew himself up to his full height, wiggled his toes, leaned forward and back on the balls of his feet, hands clasped in the small of his back, and muttered oh-so-quietly: 'There lies the difference between a professional and an amateur…'

'It was invisible,' said Holmes. 'Buried in the mud. I only saw it because I was looking for it.'

'What! You expected to find it?!' exclaimed Gregory.

'What did I tell you?' whispered Archie in my ear.

'Well, I thought it likely.'

'There you go…'

Holmes took the boots from the bag and compared the impressions of each of them with marks upon the ground. Then he clambered up to the rim of the hollow and crawled about among the ferns and bushes.

'I am afraid there are no more tracks,' said the Inspector. 'I have examined the ground very carefully for a hundred yards in each direction.'

'Indeed?' said Holmes, rising, 'Then I should not have the impertinence to do it again after what you say. But I should like to take a little walk over the moors before it grows dark, that I may know my ground tomorrow, and I think that I shall put the horseshoe into my pocket for luck.'

Colonel Tosser, who had shown some signs of impatience at my companion's quiet and systematic method of work, glanced at his watch.

'I wish you would come back with me, Inspector,' said he. 'There are several points on which I should like your advice, and especially as to whether we do not owe it to the public to remove our horse's name from the entries to the St. Leger.'

Withdraw Rampant Rod? Was he kidding us? Holmes and I would lose everything! Things looked the same for Archie who jumped so violently that I though he was going to take off, but just as he was about to ejaculate, mouth agog, Sherlock Holmes beat him to it.

'No! Certainly not!' cried Holmes, with determination. 'You must let the name stand.'

'Hear, hear!' shouted Archie.

Why was my chum so enthusiastic? I stared at him, standing next to Tosser, but he caught my eye and looked away.

The Colonel bowed. 'I am very glad to have had your opinion, sir,' said he. 'You will find us at poor Straker's house when you have finished your walk, and we can drive together to Tavistock. Come, Inspector…'

Inspector Gregory sighed and gave us a look – I could tell that he was reluctant to leave our cabal – but he succumbed to pressure and made ready to follow the Colonel with one parting remark. 'Tosser is a very big nob in these parts.'

Having not seen Colonel Tosser's nob, this is something we could not and did not wish to dispute. We nodded in unison and off he went. Holmes, Archie, and I looked at each other.

'Archie,' said I, 'how much have you at risk on the outcome of our investigation into the disappearance of Rampant Rod?'

'How very perspicacious of you,' said he. 'Dammit, do I look that obvious? Well, it isn't just money; I shall lose my honour and reputation as well. I would never recover.'

All three of us nodded in unison. Archie followed on: 'You are the one man in the country who can find Rampant Rod, Mister Holmes. Why do you think I showed up at sparrow fart this morning?

'I believe you are acquainted with this Fitzroy Simpson, are you not?'

Archie nodded.

'Then it is all three of us who are certain of ruination should I fail to succeed with this investigation,' remarked Holmes and flashed his eyes at me – he was testing Archie!

I nodded and Archie flinched, because, dear adventure-enthusiast, he didn't tell us in which way he would be affected by a successful recovery of Rampant Rod. His flinch confirmed to Holmes and me that he had backed Dessie, the second favourite, at long odds and we must keep him by our side at all times.

* * *

We walked slowly across the moor. The sun was beginning to sink behind the stables of Capleton, and the long sloping plain in front of us was tinged with gold, deepening into rich, ruddy brown where the faded ferns and brambles caught the evening light. But the glories of the landscape were all wasted upon my companion, who was sunk in the deepest thought.

'It is this way, Watson,' he said, at last. 'We may leave the question of who killed John Straker for the moment and confine ourselves to finding out what has become of the horse. Now, supposing that he broke away during or after the tragedy, where could he have gone to? The horse is a very gregarious creature. If left to him, his instincts would have been either to return to King's Pyland or go over to Capleton. Why should he run wild upon the moor? He would surely have been seen by now. And why should the gypsies kidnap him? These people always clear out when they hear of trouble, for they do not wish to be pestered by the Boys in Blue. They could not hope to sell such a horse. They would run a great risk and gain nothing by taking him. Surely that is clear.'

'Where is he then, Clever-clogs?'

'Clever-clogs? Why don't you wash your ears out, Watson? I have already said that he must have gone to King's Pyland or Capleton. Obviously, we take that as a working hypothesis and see what it leads to. This part of the moor, as the Inspector remarked, is very hard and dry. But it falls away towards Capleton, and you can see from here that there is a long hollow over yonder, which must have been very wet on Monday night. If our supposition is correct, then the horse must have crossed that, and there is the point where we should look for his tracks.'

We had been walking briskly during this conversation, with Archie as an outlier to my right. His ears were pricked – he could hear every word we said – but his face was a wall of impassiveness. A few more minutes brought us to the hollow in question. At Holmes's request I walked down the bank to the right, and to the left, but I had not taken fifty paces before I heard him give a shout and saw him waving his hand to me. The tracks of a horse were plainly outlined in the soft earth in front of him, and the shoe which he took from his pocket exactly fitted the impression.

'It's Cinderella!' cried Archie.

'Ha, Colonel, so true! See the value of imagination, Watson?' said Holmes, the condescending patrician, pointing at me whilst tapping the side of his head with his spare index finger.

'Imagination is one thing which Inspector Gregory lacks,' exclaimed I.

'And his luncheon, Watson! We imagined what might have happened, acted upon the supposition, and find ourselves justified. Let us proceed.'

We crossed the marshy bottom and passed over a quarter of a mile of dry, hard turf. I walked with Archie, quite separate from the great detective who had his eyes glued to the ground – searching, searching, searching like a schoolboy who had lost his marbles.

'I say Boner, your friend is a bloodhound!' said Archie.

'He is both a scent and sight hound. And he also has a dog's hearing, so stop calling me Boner. He does not know how the name came about in Kabul, nor do I want him to.'

*Archie had no investigative skills whatsoever.
He would make a useless detective!*

Archie chuckled to himself. 'Sorry, old chap, I cannot help myself. If your chum has such a brilliant mind, he will work that out for himself. Otherwise, I suppose the damage is done…' He chuckled to himself, the fatuous git, and slapped me on the shoulder. '*Tant pis,* as the Frogs say!'

'*Et un grand bugger off à toi*!' And we belly-laughed, as old army chums do.

Again, the ground sloped and again we came upon the tracks. We came together with Sherlock Holmes and hunted as a team. We lost the indentations for half a mile, only to pick them up once more, quite close to Capleton. I picked them out first, and I stood pointing with a look of triumph upon my face because I identified a man's footprints beside those of the horse.

'The horse was alone before,' I cried.

'You have Apache blood in the family, Watson!'

I smiled at him. Then I noticed the double track turned sharp off and took the direction of King's Pyland.

'Hallo, what is this?' I cried out.

Holmes followed along after it. His eyes were on the trail, but I happened to look a little to one side and saw to my surprise the same tracks coming back again in the opposite direction, which I pointed out to my companion.

'Another one for you, Geronimo!' chirruped Holmes.

'Thank God I did. I have saved us one hell of a long walk which would have brought us back the way we had come.'

Holmes and Archie sensed my anxiety and chuckled at me as we followed the return track. We had not gone far when it ended at the paving of asphalt which led up to the gates of the Capleton stables. As we approached a groom ran out from them.

'You lot, shoo! Fuck off out of here!' barked he.

Holmes raised his brows at the colourful language. 'I only wished to ask a question,' said he, with his finger and thumb in his waistcoat pocket, lifting a half crown into the yokel's view. It was mine, from the sideboard that morning. 'Should I be too early to see my old friend, Mister Silas Brown, if I were to call at five o'clock tomorrow morning?'

The man's face fell like a coastal landslide. 'Bless you, sir, I must beg your forgiveness! I took you for a loiterer when you are obviously an acquaintance of my master. Here he is right now, to answer your questions for himself.'

Suddenly a fierce-looking elderly man strode out from the gate with a hunting-crop swinging in his hand.

'What's this, Dawson?' he cried. 'No gossiping! Go about your business!'

The man cracked the crop across the foul-mouthed yokel with a juicy slap. The groom ran off, away from the angry man. Oh, how we all laughed in silence!

'And you?' bawled the new arrival. 'What the devil do you want round here?'

'Ten minutes' talk with you, my good sir,' said Holmes, in the sweetest of voices.

'Well, I've not time to speak to some down-from-town woolly wooftah like you. We want no strangers here. Be off with you, or you may find a dog at your heels.'

Holmes smiled. He leaned forward and whispered something in the trainer's ear. He started violently and flushed to the temples.

'It's a lie!' he shouted. 'An infernal lie!'

'Very good! We shall argue about it here in public, or talk it over in your parlour?'

The man's eyes bulged at the suggestion and, suddenly, he made a small bow to the great detective.

'Oh, please come in, sir, if you wish to…'

'I shall not keep you more than a few minutes, Watson, Colonel,' he said, turning to look at us, as smug as a pug. 'Now, Mister Brown, I am quite at your disposal.'

It was quite twenty minutes, and the red had faded into greys before Holmes and the trainer reappeared. Never have I seen such a change as had been brought about in Silas Brown in that short time. His face was ashy pale, beads of perspiration shone upon his brow. His bullying, overbearing manner was all gone too, and he cringed along at my companion's side like a dog with its master. Sherlock Holmes held the hunting-crop now, which he wagged like a branch in the wind.

'Your instructions will be done. It shall be done,' said Brown.

'There must be no mistake,' said Holmes, slapping the fine end of the crop in the palm of his hand. Brown winced as he read menace in his eyes.

'Oh, no, there shall be no mistake. It shall be there. Should I change it first or not?'

Holmes thought a little and then burst out laughing.

'No, don't,' said he. 'I shall write to you about it. No tricks now or…'. He pointed the crop at Silas Brown.

'Oh, you can trust me, you can trust me!' said the trainer earnestly, his hands up in self-defence, then turning to face the Colonel and me. 'All of you! You can rely upon me.'

Holmes slapped the crop hard across the trainer's buttocks. There was a hell of a crack of leather against jodhpur! Silas Brown shouted out loud, such was the pain!

'You must deliver the horse on the day as if it were your own,' insisted Holmes.

'Yes, I shall! I promise!'

'Good!' said Holmes, returning the riding-crop to the trembling hand of its owner. 'Well, you shall hear from me tomorrow.'

Holmes turned upon his heel and we set off for King's Pyland.

'A more perfect compound of the bully, coward and sneak than Mister Silas Brown I have seldom met with,' remarked Holmes, as we trudged along together.

'The perfect racehorse trainer then, Holmes. You remember that frightful pleb we met at Lord Coventry's last Ascot? He was a racehorse trainer. What was his name? Sanders? No... Hmm... Blanders! Yes, that was it. Colonel Blanders.'*

'Steady on, chaps, that is yet another colonel in this coterie!' remarked Archie.

'They are common as muck, Archie,' said I, then turning to Holmes. 'Brown has the horse then?'

'Yes.'

---

* see *The Adventure of The Engineer's Tongue*

*Holmes had been a prefect at Westminster school.
He knew how to dish out six of the best!*

'WHAT DID I SAY?!' shouted Archie. 'I expounded my theorem called "the bloody obvious" only an hour ago and I was shot down!'

'Mister Brown fooled the police,' said Holmes, 'not a difficult thing to do with a horse when you are an old horse-faker like him. Naturally, he tried to bluster out of it, but I described to him so exactly what his actions had been upon that morning, that he is convinced that I was watching him. Of course, you observed the peculiarly square toes in the impressions, and that his own boots exactly corresponded to them. Again, of course, no subordinate would have dared to have done such a thing. I described to him how when, according to his custom, he was the first down, he perceived a strange horse wandering over the moor; he went out to it, and his astonishment recognising from the enormous penis which has given the favourite of the St. Leger its name that chance put in his power the only horse which could beat the one upon which he had put his money. Then I described how his first impulse had been to lead him back to King's Pyland, and how the devil had shown him how he could hide the horse until the race was over, and how he had led it back and concealed it at Capleton. When I told him every detail, he gave it up and thought only of saving his own skin.'

'Just like Colonel Blanders!' said I.

'Indeed, Watson, indeed… But at least we have found the horse now.'

'Hu-zzah…' said Archie, all lacklustre, and then looked embarrassed, like he wished he hadn't said anything.

'You seem to be displeased, Colonel?' inquired Holmes inquisitively.

Archie was taken aback by Holmes's sharpness. 'Oh, I meant it. Oh, to be a detective... Huzzah!'

My chum was covering up for his outburst. He had no more intention of taking up private investigation than I had in holy orders. He was up to something, but I couldn't quite put my finger on what it was. I could see that Holmes was suspicious, so I distracted him. After all, it was bound to reflect badly upon me and I wanted to clear the air with Archie later, in private.

'Surely you should not leave the horse in his power now,' said I to the great detective, 'since he has every interest in injuring it?'

'My dear, Watson, he will guard it like his own grandchild. He knows that his only hope of mercy is to produce it safely for the St. Leger.'

'Colonel Tosser did not impress me as a man who would be likely to show much mercy.'

'The matter of mercy does not rest with Colonel Tosser. I follow my own methods. I shall tell him as much or as little as I choose. That is the advantage of being unofficial. I don't know whether you observed it, Watson, but the Colonel's manner has been just a trifle cavalier to me. I am inclined to have a little amusement at his expense. Say nothing to him about me finding Rampant Rod.'

'Not a chance, Holmes,' said I, noting the way he said "me" instead of "us." 'Certainly not!.'

'Nor you, Colonel Tugwell. Do not utter a word.'

Archie inclined his head in acknowledgement.

'Of course,' said Holmes, 'this is all quite a minor case compared with the question of who killed John Straker.'

'And you will devote yourself now to that?'

'On the contrary, we both go back to London by the night train.'

I was thunderstruck by my friend's words! We had only been a few hours in Devonshire, and that he should give up an investigation which he had begun so brilliantly was quite incomprehensible to me. Not a word more could I draw from him until we were back at the trainer's house. Colonel Tosser and Inspector Gregory were awaiting us in the parlour, a large county cream tea spread out in front of them, a large proportion of which was descending the policeman's gullet.

'My friend and I return to town by the midnight express,' said Holmes. 'We have had a charming little breath of your beautiful Dartmoor air.'

The Inspector gawped like a bullfrog mid-mouthful. Tosser's lips curled in a sneer.

'So, you despair of arresting the murderer of poor Straker,' said he.

Holmes shrugged his shoulders. 'There are certainly grave difficulties in the way,' said he. 'I have every hope, however, that your horse will start upon Tuesday, and I beg that you will have your jockey in readiness. Might I ask for a photograph of Mister John Straker?'

The Inspector took one from an envelope in his pocket and handed it to him.

'My dear Gregory, you anticipate all my wants. If I might ask you to wait here for an instant, I have a question which I should like to put to the widow.'

'She is upstairs, sitting vigil next to her husband,' said Gregory.

Sherlock Holmes disappeared up the stairs.

'I must say I am rather disappointed in our London consultant,' said Colonel Tosser, bluntly, as my friend left the room. 'I do not see that we are any further than when he arrived.'

'At least you have the assurance that your horse will run,' said I.

'Yes, I have his assurance' said the Colonel, with a shrug of his shoulders. 'I should prefer to have the horse here at my side.'

I was about to make a quip along the lines of him already having a greedy pig by his side when Holmes descended the staircase and entered the room again.

'Now, gentlemen,' said he, 'I am quite ready for Tavistock.' Then he threw me a slantindicular glance that told me in no uncertain terms that he had uncovered a fact of critical importance during his diversion upstairs. Talking of which, I noticed Archie bounding up them as fast as his legs would carry him. What was he up to?

We walked out of the house and stepped into the carriage parked immediately outside the door. One of the stable lads held the door open for us. A sudden idea seemed to occur to Holmes, for he leaned forward and touched the lad upon the sleeve.

'You have a few sheep in the paddock,' he said. 'Who attends to them?'

'I do, sir.'

'Have you noticed anything amiss of them of late?'

'Well, sir, not of much account, but three of them have gone lame, sir.'

I could see that Holmes was extremely pleased, for he chuckled and rubbed his hands together.

'That was a long shot, Watson; a very long shot!' said he, pinching my arm.

'Gregory, let me recommend to your attention this singular epidemic among the sheep.' Holmes became restless, looking side to side, as if someone or something was missing.

'Now, it is time to leave, but we cannot do so without your friend. It is essential he comes with us. Where is he, Watson?'

'I last saw him climbing the staircase, Holmes.'

'Quite so!' chuckled he, with a mischievous look upon his face. 'We need to keep him close by because he has backed the second favourite in the St. Leger. Leave him on his own down here and we might find Rampant Rod has developed a sweet tooth. I think it an excellent idea for you to go and fetch him.'

He directed my eyes discreetly upwards to a first-floor bedroom window. I followed northward until they rested upon... Oh, my God! It was Archie and the widow Straker mounted, going at it hammer and tongs! She was bent over, her skirt thrown up over her back, as he galloped away like Wild Bill, thrusting like a steam hammer! For a moment I was mesmerised, such was the shock at the gloriously primordial sight, and then Holmes kicked my ankle. I glanced down and was relieved to see the Colonel and the Inspector were oblivious to the coupling above them and still enquiring of the great detective about his Rampant Rod observations. I looked back up. Archie was reaching the climax of his performance; the widow Straker was in the throes of ecstasy, her arms twirling like a windmill! Then, they had finished. I glanced at my half hunter. Good! If we didn't delay longer, we could still catch the last train to London. I grabbed the door handle of the coach and ran out shouting: 'I'll get him!'

By the time I had run upstairs, urged my naked friend into his tweeds and returned to the carriage Holmes was confirming the relevance of the sheep to Gregory. He gave me a "I told you so" raise of his brows, and he smirked.

'One more thing, Mister Holmes,' said the Inspector, 'is there any other point to which you would wish to draw my attention?'

'Yes. To the curious incident of the dog in the night-time.'

'The dog did nothing in the night-time.'

'That was the curious incident,' remarked Sherlock Holmes.

The two men looked dumbfounded, as if they had been shot.

'Drive on!' cried Holmes.

As the carriage set off Archie threw his arms out wide. 'Sorry, chaps! The dog demanded a bone, and who am I to deny a damsel in distress?'

* * *

Four days later Holmes and I were again in the rain bound for Doncaster, to see the race for the St Leger. As instructed by Sherlock Holmes himself, I had been busy raising funds to wager on Rampant Rod and then trundling over to the Old Kent Road to make the bets with our chosen turf accountant.

'Watson, what liability do we have now with Nasty Nige?'

'I have hocked anything we hold in our possession with old Prawn Balls* down the road, items of the most microscopic value, even if we don't own them. The Azerbaijani prayer mat; your sapphire tie-pin and cufflinks; my grandmother's silver tea service; your brother Mycroft's copy of the First Folio, left with you for safe-keeping; the two Constables and the dodgy Rembrandt; your stamp collection and my cabinet of ancient wax seals; ninety guineas escrowed as a legal charge by one of our clients, The Maharajah of Oranjeboom; and last, but not least, the cash contents of Missus Hudson's safe.'

'Which I opened for you.'

'Yes, and we now have only two days to replace it. I heard that she would return a day sooner from visiting her bulldog of a sister than we were told.'

'If that horse doesn't turn up for the Leger, Watson, we are ruined. And we are homeless. What price on the tissue?'

'I did well, Holmes. Nifty was very suspicious when I wanted to back a horse that had gone missing. But he doesn't really know me, so when I acted like I was out with the fairies...'

'Easy for you, Watson.'

'Like I was light on grey matter and testosterone, he took two hundred at five-to-one, two-twenty-five at eleven-to-two and a cool monkey at six-to-one, the last being Missus Hudson's unwitting contribution.'

'Good, Watson. When Rampant Rod storms home we enrich ourselves with a handsome return of five

---
* Cruikshank's Pawnbrokers, of Drury Lane

thousand, nine hundred and seventy-nine guineas and ten shillings.'

'Indeed so, Holmes, we become men of means.'

Colonel Tosser met us, by appointment, meter running, outside the station, and we drove in his drag to the course beyond the town. His face was grave, and his manner was cold in the extreme.

'I have seen nothing of my horse,' said he.

'I suppose you would know him when you saw him?' asked Holmes.

The Colonel was already tense and now he turned angry.

'I have been on the turf for twenty years and never was asked such an impertinent question as that before! A retarded guinea-pig would know Rampant Rod with his white forehead and mottled off fore-leg.'

Sherlock Holmes disregarded Tosser's childish reference to the harmless rodent.

'How is the betting?'

'Well, that is the curious part of it,' said he. 'You could have got ten to one yesterday, but the price has become shorter and shorter, until you can hardly get two to one now.'

'Ho-hum!' said Holmes, smiling at me like Carroll's Cheshire Cat.

'Somebody knows something, that is for sure,' said I, stifling a muffled laugh. Over the last couple of days, we had backed the Colonel's horse all around town. Arche had cleared out his bank account, gathered up all his available assets and, together with his Purdeys, had hocked the lot in Drury Lane and backed Rampant Rod at tens and nines all the way home.

'I hope so... because that is not the only reason that I am in a black mood. 'Your friend, that Colonel Tugwell? Have you any idea of what he was up to with the widow Straker? Hmm? Why is he not with you?'

Oh dear! Tosser knew about Archie's carnal assignation. However, he didn't know what Holmes and I knew after Archie had spilled the beans to us on the journey back into town from Dartmoor a few days ago. I was tongue-tied – I didn't like to say anything – but, by good fortune, that was the moment the drag drew up in the enclosure near the racecourse grandstand. We were faced by the board listing the St. Leger entries and state of the betting market. Colonel Tosser digested the information and nearly wet himself.

'Why, what is going on?' cried Tosser. 'Rampant Rod is favourite!'

'Look at that Holmes!' I cried. 'The Rod is now five to four on. Dessie has drifted to seven to two.'

'My horse is running!' exclaimed the Colonel as he jumped down from his seat. But he wasn't very happy; in fact, he was highly agitated. 'Where is my horse? I can see the runners for the race, but I cannot see my colours! They have not passed by. WHERE IS HE?'

As he shouted, a powerful bay horse swept out from the weighing enclosure and cantered past us, bearing on his back the well-known black and red quarters of the Colonel.

'There he is, sir!' cried Holmes, sweeping his arm gracefully towards the bay.

'That's not my horse!' cried Tosser. Many people in our vicinity stopped and stared because the Colonel was a well-known figure in racing circles, and he was most agitated. They listened as he ranted on about the horse bearing his colours not having a white hair on its body and, therefore, it could not be his animal. 'That is not my horse!' was his repetition.

Holmes grabbed me by the sleeve and whispered in my ear. 'Watson, we have everything we own in the world riding on the back of this loudmouth's horse. You go down to the ring and check on the market whilst I silence this oaf.'

'He is going to ruin everything if we don't shut him up. Uh-oh, Holmes... Here come the stewards.'

As I toddled off towards Tattersalls, I glanced over my shoulder at the moment when the frock-coated officials had demanded an explanation from the Colonel. Just as he was about to land us in it, Sherlock Holmes came from behind and accidentally kicked him in the rear of the knee. Tosser collapsed onto the ground like a felled tree and writhed in pain. The great detective made mock entreaties of assistance. Perfect!

Down in the ring the bookies were going mad for Rampant Rod, the price tumbling to seven to-four on. When the race started, I had reported back to Holmes. Colonel Tosser was gazing through his field glasses.

'Capital! My horse has had an excellent start!' he cried. 'They are coming round the bend and my boy is up with the pace.'

We had a superb view as they came up the long straight at Doncaster. The six horses were so close together that Mrs. Straker's knickers would have covered them. Halfway up the straight Dessie went into the lead.

'Dammit, Holmes! I cried. 'If this doesn't change, we will have to make a run for it!'

'We are heading for a debtors' jail, Watson. Two years of purgatory, and the most depraved degradation that a human being can imagine. But hold on! They still have two furlongs to go and look!'

Suddenly Dessie was tiring. His bolt was shot, and the Colonel's horse had taken wings and was flying down the straight towards us. By the time it passed the lollipop it was a good four lengths in front of its nearest rival. Relief flooded over!

'I win! I have won the Leger!' cried Tosser, dancing from one foot to another in a most ungentlemanly way. My word, he was showing his true colours, a revelation that was met with raised brows all around us. 'Goodness knows with what horse... but I'm still the winner! You are losers!'

Holmes smiled at me and declared: 'Not us, Watson. We are big winners!'

And Nifty Nigel was the biggest loser of all.

* * *

We had the corner of a Pullman car to ourselves that evening as we whirled back to London, and I fancy that the journey was as short a one to Colonel Tosser as to myself, as we listened to our companion's narrative of the events which had occurred at the Dartmoor training stables upon that dramatic night, and how he had unravelled them.

'Mister Holmes,' barked the Colonel, 'I am still fixated by the image in the unsaddling stalls when you rubbed down Rod's coat with white wine and all of his marks which distinguish him reappeared. What a moment that was! The looks upon my fellow owners and friends will stay with me the rest of my years.'

It was obvious that Colonel Tosser was a self-made man!

'As will your dancing,' said Holmes.

We burst into spontaneous laughter. Yes, even Tosser was relaxed and genial now that he had recovered his horse and won the race. Ah, how life became so gay when the bookmakers paid for it!

'Yes, you are correct in your observation there too, Mister Holmes. I wouldn't win any prizes for my dancing ability. But enough about me. I would like to know how your investigation became successful.'

Holmes chuckled to himself. 'I have told you already the identity of John Straker's killer, and why he was brought down to earth, but my methods are catalogued by my companion here, Doctor Watson. He may choose to chronicle this affair.'

'Certainly, I shall!' I replied. 'It is worthy, Holmes, but I cannot make a start until I know precisely what happened.'

Holmes acknowledged with a facial tick, as if he had farted silently.

'That, Watson, can be delivered to you at a later date.'

The Colonel leaned forward in his seat. 'In which case, gentlemen, for that information to be delivered right now, as we sit here, I shall render to you the sum of five hundred pounds in grateful acknowledgement of your services to me.'

'No, Colonel Tosser,' said Holmes, 'that will not be...'

'We accept!' said I. 'Holmes, you may begin...'

Sherlock Holmes gave me a momentary stare but then resigned himself to telling the true story. 'I confess,' said he, 'that any theories which I had formed from the newspaper reports were entirely erroneous. And yet there were indications there, had they not been overlaid by other details which concealed their true importance. I went to Devonshire with the conviction that Fitzroy Simpson was the true culprit, although of course, I saw that the evidence against him was by no means complete.'

'It was while I was in the carriage, just as we reached the trainer's house, that the immense significance of the curried mutton occurred to me. You may remember that when we completed our journey to the house I was distracted and remained sitting after you had all alighted. I was marvelling in my own mind how I could possibly have overlooked so obvious a clue.'

'I confess,' said the Colonel, 'that even now I cannot see how a lamb curry helps us.'

'It was the first link in my chain of reasoning. Powdered opium is by no means tasteless. The flavour is not disagreeable, but it is perceptible. Was it mixed with any ordinary dish, the eater would undoubtedly detect it, and would probably eat no more? A curry was exactly the medium which would disguise this taste of the opium. It was infeasible that this stranger, Fitzroy Simpson, could have caused lamb curry to be served in the trainer's family that night, and it is surely too monstrous a coincidence to suppose that he happened to come along with powdered opium upon the very night when a dish happened to be served. That is unthinkable. Therefore, Simpson becomes eliminated from the case, and our attention centres upon Straker and his wife, the only two people who could have chosen a curry for supper that night. The opium was added after the dish was set aside for the stable boy, for the others had the same for supper with no ill effects.

Which of them, then, had access to that dish without the maid seeing them? The answer is John Straker.'

'Before deciding that query I had grasped the significance of the silence of the dog, for one true inference invariably suggest the others. The Simpson incident had shown me that a dog was kept in the stables, and yet, though someone had been in and fetched out a horse, he had not barked enough to arouse the two lads in the loft. Obviously, the midnight visitor was someone whom the dog knew well.'

'I was already convinced, or almost convinced, that John Straker went down to the stables in the dead of night and took out Rampant Rod. For what purpose? For a dishonest one, obviously, or why should he drug his own stable boy? And yet I was at a loss to know why. There have been cases before now where trainers have made sure of great sums of money by laying against their own horses, through agents, and then prevented them from winning by fraud. Sometimes a jockey pulls a horse by sleight of hand, other times by more subtle means. What had occurred here? I hoped that the contents of his pockets might help me to form a conclusion.'

'And they did so. You cannot have forgotten the singular knife, which was found in the dead man's hand, a knife which certainly no sane man would choose for a weapon. It was, as Doctor Watson told us, a form of knife which is used for the most delicate operations in surgery. And I concluded that it was to be used for a delicate operation that night. You must know, with your wide experience of turf matters, Colonel Tosser, that it is possible to make a slight nick upon the tendon of a horse's ham, and to do it subcutaneously so as to leave absolutely no trace. A horse so treated would develop a slight lameness which would be put down to a strain in exercise or a touch of rheumatism, but never to foul play.'

'Straker would do that? cried Tosser. 'The villain! The scoundrel!'

'It is why John Straker wished to take the horse out on to the moor. So spirited a creature would have roused the soundest of sleepers when it felt the prick of the knife. It was absolutely necessary to do it in the open air.'

'I have been blind!' moaned the Colonel. 'Of course, that was why he needed the candle, and struck the match.'

'Undoubtedly. But in examining his belongings, I was fortunate to discover, not only the method of the crime, but even its motive. As a man of the world, Colonel, you must know that men do not carry other people's bills about in their pockets. It is trouble enough to settle our own, so I concluded that Straker was leading a double life and keeping a second establishment. The nature of the bill showed that there was a lady in the case, and one who had expensive tastes. Liberal as you are with your servants, one hardly expects that they can buy twenty-guinea walking dresses for their women. I questioned Missus Straker as to the dress without her knowing it and having satisfied myself that it had never been given to her, I made a note of the milliner's address. When I called there with Straker's photograph, I could easily establish that Missus Darbyshire and John Straker were entwined, and she was an expensive luxury.'

'From that time on all was plain. Straker had led out the horse to a hollow where his light would be invisible. Simpson, in his flight, had dropped his cravat, and Straker had picked it up with some idea, perhaps, that he might use it in securing the horse's leg. Once in the hollow he had got behind the horse, and had struck a light, but the creature, frightened at the sudden glare, and with the strange instinct of animals feeling that some mischief was intended, had lashed out, and the steel shoe on Rampant Rod's hoof, attached to one of the most athletic hind legs in racing bloodstock, had struck Straker full on the forehead. He was dead before his body fell to the ground and his knife gashed his thigh on the way down. Colonel Tosser, does that satisfy your thirst for an explanation to this investigation?'

'Wonderful!' cried the Colonel. 'Absolutely wonderful! You might have been there.'

'My final shot was, I confess, a very long one. It struck me that so astute a man as Straker would not undertake this delicate tendon-nicking without a little practice. What could he practise on? My eyes fell upon the sheep, and I asked a question, which, rather to my surprise, showed that my surmise was correct.'

'As always, Holmes!' I expounded, thumping my fist upon my knee to emphasise his detective ability and persuade Tosser to remit the five hundred pounds. 'Colonel?'

Tosser gave me an inquisitive stare before the penny dropped. 'You have made it perfectly clear, Mister Holmes' said he, reaching into his pocket and extracting his wallet. He held it aloft. 'I have a couple of queries, Mister Holmes... Where was the horse?'

'The horse bolted after it killed Straker. It was cared for by one of your neighbours.'

'I shall overlook pursuing that chapter of this mystery any further, bearing in mind the circumstances.' Tosser leaned forward and his eyes narrowed... 'But lastly, what about Colonel Tugwell? He abused Missus Straker and I wish to get my hands on him!'

'You should be shaking his hand instead, Colonel. If it hadn't been for Watson's army chum uncovering the urgent carnal needs of the widow Straker, I wouldn't have been certain that her husband was having an affair with Missus Darbyshire. Unlike Rampant Rod's future life at stud, his trainer could not even keep two old mares satisfied. For Colonel Tugwell to conjoin so easily with Missus Straker, she had to be desperate.'

Sherlock Holmes's theory held no water. Women from all walks of life were happy to be conjoined with Archie; in fact, they questioned their allure if he ignored them. Still, I decided to say nothing and leave him in his bubble of self-belief.

'Well, bless my soul, let us raise a toast to Colonel Tugwell!' Tosser laughed and let us in on a secret. 'I have to say, gentlemen, and let us keep this between ourselves, I had a go myself and she was no great shake of the leg. I'll let her go.'

The dirty dog! Holmes and I raised brows and pondered the moment...

'This is Kings Cross station and the end of our journey,' cried Holmes. 'Accompany me to Baker Street and I shall deliver him into your hands.'

'I accept!' cried our unsolicited client and offered the sheaf of fifty ten-pound notes to the great detective, which I intercepted *en route* in my upturned hat.

* * *

Sherlock Holmes insisted we enter 221B from the Baker Street pavement in the utmost silence. Then, he indicated we should creep up the staircase catlike, applying pressure daintily to each tread with a crimped foot. I spent the journey up the wooden hill adding up our winnings and, eventually, gave up. It was enough to keep us in clover and fine claret for many a long winter.

When we entered the apartment all was quiet. My companion indicated we should keep it that way. We settled our guest with a glass of Warres '78 and a Sobranie Sub Rosa, which he took up joyfully and inhaled deeply.

'Now, Mister Holmes,' said he in a whisper. 'I have fulfilled my side of our arrangement. Perhaps you would do the honour of doing the same for me?'

'It will be my pleasure, Colonel,' said Holmes. He raised himself up from his chair and ambled over to the small landing where my bedroom was. Why would he be heading towards my room? To my surprise, he twisted the handle of my door and pushed it open.

'There!' he cried. 'There is your man, Colonel!'

We peered into my room only to be introduced to the spectacle of my army chum's bum laying snugly between the shapely thighs of my landlady, entwined-divine, *in flagrante*. He had the grace to stop and look over his shoulder. Colonel Tosser laughed and pointed with his fat Turkish. 'I believe every word you told me, Mister Holmes!'

'I say, Boner, old fruit, The Rod made it, eh? I picked up a mountain of cash from Sir Gaylon and when Missus H wandered by, I really had no choice but to requisition your billet for emergency services!'

Sherlock Holmes bowed his head and then caught my eye. 'It must be quite an accolade, Doctor Watson, to have a nickname like that. My congratulations to you.'

Archie raised himself again from Mrs Hudson. 'Have you deduced, Mister Holmes, where Boner comes from?'

'Why, yes, naturally I have. It can only be his prowess with...'

I stepped into the doorway, blocking off the happy couple from the great detective.

'THAT is enough of that, thank you, gentlemen!' I pulled the door closed as quickly as possible, just as Mrs. Hudson followed up with: 'Oh Archie, you are making me ovulate...'

I locked the door with my key. Aghast at the insult of my bed being defiled yet again for casual intercourse.[*]

---

[*] see *The Case of the Randy Stepfather*